The Story of Chinaman's Hat
Written and Illustrated by Dean Howell

Produced and Published by
Island Heritage Publishing
Copyright © 1990 Island Heritage Publishing
First Edition, Seventeenth Printing, 2006
ISBN No. 0-89610-149-5

Address orders and editorial correspondence to:

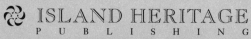 ISLAND HERITAGE
P U B L I S H I N G
94-411 KŌʻAKI STREET, WAIPAHU, HAWAIʻI 96797
ORDERS: (800) 468-2800 • INFORMATION: (808) 564-8800
FAX: (808) 564-8877 • www.islandheritage.com

The Story of
Chinaman's Hat

WRITTEN AND ILLUSTRATED BY
DEAN HOWELL

In the sunny Chinese village of Shin Hway lived a boy named Lick Bean and a girl named Mei Mei. They were very good friends.

Shin Hway was famous for its hats made of bamboo and Mei Mei learned the art of hat-making when she was very young. She practiced and practiced, making hat after hat, until she finally made one that was equal to the finest hats in China. This hat she gave to her friend Lick Bean.

Lick Bean loved the hat made by Mei Mei. Though he was smaller than the other boys his age, wearing his special hat made him feel tall and proud.

As they grew older, other boys wanted Mei Mei's friendship and they tried to impress her by showing off. Some of the boys did tricks and tumbles which Lick Bean knew he could never do. Mei Mei giggled as one of the boys walked on his hands to entertain her. Lick Bean crept away sadly. He had never felt so small and weak.

As Lick Bean wandered slowly through the market, he saw the Fong Family Herb Shop. He knew that herbs could make you well if you were sick and today Lick Bean felt sick and sad. 'Maybe,' he thought, 'Mr. Fong will have an herb to make me feel happy.'

"Happy herbs?" laughed Mr. Fong. "No, but I could tell you a few jokes." He told jokes but Lick Bean didn't even smile.

"Your face is making me sad," said Mr. Fong. "What makes a young man so unhappy that he doesn't laugh at my jokes?"

Lick Bean told him about the bigger boys. "If I could just grow some, and be stronger, I could walk on my hands and make Mei Mei laugh, too."

"Well if your size is the problem, maybe I do have something for you," said Mr. Fong. As he took a box from his shelves, Mr. Fong said, "The powder in this box is made from the ground-up roots of a giant tree from a faraway land. These trees are almost as tall as the mountains. Just a little of this powder, made into a tea, will make you grow." Mr. Fong gave Lick Bean the whole box! "Be careful not to drink too much at once," Mr. Fong cautioned.

Lick Bean practically flew home. Now he would grow, he thought.
"It's magic tea mom! Can you make some?"

"Well, I think your father should look at the tea first," said his mother.

But Lick Bean didn't listen to his mother, and he didn't listen to Mr. Fong either as he poured all the powder into a cup and ladled some water over the brown dust. It looked like mud, but Lick Bean held his nose and gulped it down. In a moment his body began to feel different.

It seemed like his clothes were shrinking. They got tighter and tighter. Lick Bean was growing taller and taller so fast he screamed "NO!" He didn't want to be this big, and yet the next moment he was bigger still. He grew and grew and GREW! Lick Bean was scared. He wished he had listened to his mother and Mr. Fong.

How could he walk on his hands to impress Mei Mei with such long legs to hold up in the air? Now he was not just a very skinny person, but a giant skinny person.

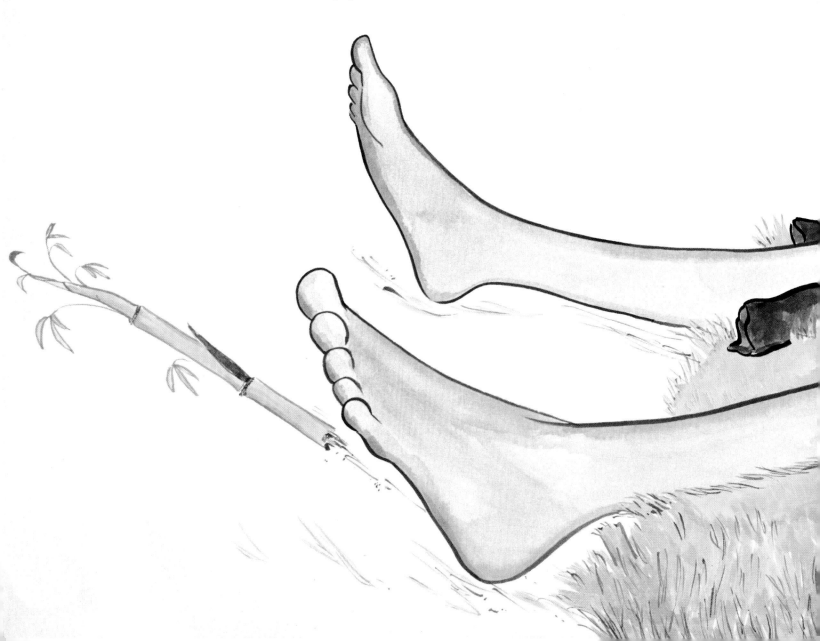

"Would Mei Mei laugh or scream if she saw me?" Lick Bean wondered as he jumped over some small hills. Lick Bean could now walk over mountains in just a few giant steps. Before he knew it, he was miles away from his village, his home, and his friend Mei Mei.

At the thought of Mei Mei, Lick Bean reached for his favorite hat. Oh! How small it was! He was glad he had not lost Mei Mei's gift to him.

Then he found something else. Some long black hairs coming from his chin. He had a beard! Was he becoming as big and as old as the tree from which the tea powder came? "Now a beard!" laughed Lick Bean, "Mei Mei would giggle if she could see this!"

Holding his tiny hat in one hand, and pulling
on his new beard with the other, Lick Bean had an
idea. He threaded one of the long black hairs
through his hat and secured it with a knot. Now he
couldn't lose it. Lick Bean ran and jumped in the
ocean. He quickly swam out where the water was
deep and black.

Suddenly feeling sleepy, he closed his eyes and was asleep in a moment. As Lick Bean slept, he was carried away by another giant, a giant ocean current. His body floated like a huge ship. Tied to his beard, his cherished hat bobbed over the waves like a child's toy.

All through the night Lick Bean's sleeping body moved swiftly through the South China Sea and into the Pacific Ocean. Powerful tides swept him along on racing waves until morning found him off a beach in the Hawaiian islands very, very far from his home.

When he stood up, Lick Bean saw many small brown people looking at him with wide eyes and open mouths. He explained who he was and how he had grown so big and the people began to smile.

Lick Bean wished he had a gift to show his friendship, but the only thing he had brought with him was his hat. Mei Mei had made it and given it to him, and so it was his favorite thing, but Lick Bean knew that giving away your favorite thing is a priceless gift. That's what Mei Mei had done when she gave him her finest hat. So Lick Bean made a difficult decision.

He untied his hat and placed it on the King's head. The King was very pleased. All of the people began to dance and sing as drums beat a happy rhythm.

The Hawaiian King wanted to give Lick Bean a very special gift
in return. "The giant should have a giant hat like the one he gave me,"
he thought. So he put his weavers to work on a giant Chinaman's hat
for Lick Bean to wear. At the same time carvers worked on a giant koa
wood bowl for Lick Bean to eat out of.

Lick Bean was so happy as he put the new giant hat on his head.
'Mei Mei would be proud,' he thought.

After he had eaten Lick Bean felt strange. He was so tired! Then, as if in slow motion, he sank below the water. First his big old body, then his long grey beard, and finally his head disappeared beneath the surface. The only thing left to see was his new giant hat, that now looked like a new little island.

Yes the magic tea had put Lick Bean to sleep. His sleep was so deep that he didn't need to breathe for a very long time as he lay beneath the surface. The Hawaiian people's hearts were broken. They thought their new friend must be dead.

Many weeks passed and the people continued to mourn for the giant who had come out of the sea. They looked out at the giant hat sitting in the bay but there was no movement, all was still and sad.

Then one day the people saw a fountain of water erupt
near the island hat — like a bubble bursting — and something
popped out of the water.

The Hawaiians jumped into their canoes and paddled out
to meet a lonely swimmer. When they brought him back to shore
the people gathered around with great curiosity.

"I guess you used to know me as a giant," said the boy. "The magic tea has lost its power. I am Lick Bean!"

The Hawaiians were overjoyed to see the real Lick Bean.

Not long after this magical day, a Chinese boat was seen in the bay. It sailed right past Lick Bean's fern covered hat. And who do you think came off the boat right behind the captain? It was Mr. Fong who had given Lick Bean the magical tea! Mr. Fong was so surprised to see his little friend. "What are you doing in Hawaii?" Lick Bean and Mr. Fong asked each other at the same time.

"I'll tell you how I got here on our way back home if you will let me come with you," said Lick Bean.

Mr. Fong laughed and said, "We are on our way back to China now. I've sailed with this ship all over the world collecting herbs, even more powder from the giant trees!"

A few days later the Chinese ship was ready to set sail. Regretfully, Lick Bean said goodbye to the Islanders and thanked them for their kindness and generosity.

As the ship left the bay, it sailed past
the giant island hat. Lick Bean couldn't believe
that huge island once sat on top of his head.
'Life is filled with amazing and wonderful
things,' he thought. As he thought this,
he jumped up and walked on his hands,
just like the bigger boys back home!

When Lick Bean arrived back home he was so excited to see his friend Mei Mei.

"Where have you been Lick Bean?" asked Mei Mei.

"I've been learning to walk on my hands," said Lick Bean.

Mei Mei thought that Lick Bean looked taller and stronger, but his size wasn't important. She was just happy to see her friend again, safe and sound.

Of course she had a gift for him, her newest and best bamboo hat.

"I'm so happy to have a new hat," said Lick Bean. "I left two very special hats in Hawaii."

Well, Lick Bean had a story to tell Mei Mei that she probably wouldn't believe, but people who see the Chinaman's Hat island in the Hawaiian bay can see for themselves the evidence of Lick Bean's visit to Hawaii. They say his giant spirit still rests beneath the island hat and plays with the whales.